Lone Shark

Anders Hanson

Illustrated by Anne Haberstroh

Consulting Editor, Diane Craig, M.A./Reading Specialist

ABDO
Publishing Company

Published by ABDO Publishing Company, 4940 Viking Drive, Edina, Minnesota 55435.

Printed in the United States.

Credits
Edited by: Pam Price
Curriculum Coordinator: Nancy Tuminelly
Cover and Interior Design and Production: Mighty Media
Photo Credits: Doug Perrine/SeaPics.com, Mark Strickland/SeaPics.com, Ron & Valerie Taylor/SeaPics.com, James D. Watt/SeaPics.com, ShutterStock

Library of Congress Cataloging-in-Publication Data

Hanson, Anders, 1980-
   Lone shark / Anders Hanson; illustrated by Anne Haberstroh.
      p. cm. -- (Fact & fiction. Critter chronicles)
   Summary: Clark, a small, young shark, is lonely until he meets just the right friend. Alternating pages provide facts about sharks and remoras.
   ISBN 10 1-59928-452-9 (hardcover)
   ISBN 10 1-59928-453-7 (paperback)

   ISBN 13 978-1-59928-452-1 (hardcover)
   ISBN 13 978-1-59928-453-8 (paperback)
   [1. Loneliness--Fiction. 2. Friendship--Fiction. 3. Sharks--Fiction. 4. Remora (Fish)--Fiction.]
 I. Haberstroh, Anne, ill. II. Title. III. Series.

   PZ7.H1982867Lon 2006
   [E]--dc22   2006005545

SandCastle Level: Fluent

SandCastle™ books are created by a professional team of educators, reading specialists, and content developers around five essential components—phonemic awareness, phonics, vocabulary, text comprehension, and fluency—to assist young readers as they develop reading skills and strategies and increase their general knowledge. All books are written, reviewed, and leveled for guided reading, early reading intervention, and Accelerated Reader® programs for use in shared, guided, and independent reading and writing activities to support a balanced approach to literacy instruction. The SandCastle™ series has four levels that correspond to early literacy development. The levels help teachers and parents select appropriate books for young readers.

Emerging Readers
(no flags)

Beginning Readers
(1 flag)

Transitional Readers
(2 flags)

Fluent Readers
(3 flags)

These levels are meant only as a guide. All levels are subject to change.

FACT & Fiction

This series provides early fluent readers the opportunity to develop reading comprehension strategies and increase fluency. These books are appropriate for guided, shared, and independent reading.

FACT The left-hand pages incorporate realistic photographs to enhance readers' understanding of informational text.

Fiction The right-hand pages engage readers with an entertaining, narrative story that is supported by whimsical illustrations.

The Fact and Fiction pages can be read separately to improve comprehension through questioning, predicting, making inferences, and summarizing. They can also be read side-by-side, in spreads, which encourages students to explore and examine different writing styles.

FACT OR Fiction? This fun quiz helps reinforce students' understanding of what is real and not real.

SPEED READ The text-only version of each section includes word-count rulers for fluency practice and assessment.

GLOSSARY Higher-level vocabulary and concepts are defined in the glossary.

SandCastle™ would like to hear from you.

Tell us your stories about reading this book. What was your favorite page? Was there something hard that you needed help with? Share the ups and downs of learning to read. To get posted on the ABDO Publishing Company Web site, send us an e-mail at:

sandcastle@abdopublishing.com

Most sharks are solitary creatures. Some sharks swim in small groups.

Clark is a small, young shark in a very big ocean. Everywhere he looks, he sees other fish frolicking and playing games together. But Clark doesn't have any friends. He feels awfully lonely.

5

Reefs are like densely populated undersea cities. This makes them great places for sharks to find meals.

As Clark passes a coral reef, he sees a lone clown fish nervously poking its head out of a crevice. Clark gathers his courage and swims over to introduce himself. "Hello, my name is Clark. Will you be my friend?" Clark asks cheerfully.

Sharks eat fish, shellfish, squid, turtles, plankton, and marine mammals.

"Most certainly not! I would never befriend a shark. One minute we'd be playfully romping about the reef, the next minute I'd wind up in your belly! No, that just wouldn't do," the clown fish declares as he ducks back inside his home.

Unlike most animals, sharks can move
both their upper and lower jaws.

Clark feels dejected, but he's still determined to find a friend. "Maybe I should smile more," he thinks. Clark shyly makes his way over to a school of tuna and gives them his biggest smile.

11

Some shark's teeth are replaced about every eight days. Certain species lose more than 50,000 teeth during their lifetime.

But at the sight of Clark's wide-open mouth filled with rows of terribly sharp teeth, the horrified tuna dart off without even a simple good-bye!

13

Sharks are often accompanied by suckerfish, called remoras, that latch onto the shark's body.

"Hmm," Clark thinks, "maybe I'm just not meant to have friends." But just then, a small, perky fish swims right up to Clark and blurts out, "Hi, my name's Laura Remora. Do you want to be my friend?"

15

The whale shark is the largest fish.
Although it has about 300 rows of tiny
teeth, it is harmless to humans.

Clark blushes with delight. "Really? I'd love to be your friend, Laura. My name's Clark." This time he tries to smile without showing his teeth so he won't frighten his new friend.

17

Remoras attach themselves to sharks for transport, protection, and an occasional free meal. They often eat parasites that harm sharks.

"Don't worry," Laura says. "You don't seem so scary to me. I bet you're the most delightful shark in the whole ocean!"

"Thanks," Clark responds. "It's so nice to finally have a good friend. If you hop on my back, I'll take you on a fantastic ride around the reef!"

19

FACT or Fiction?

Read each statement below. Then decide whether it's from the FACT section or the Fiction section!

  1. Sharks eat turtles.

  2. Sharks smile at fish they want to make friends with.

  3. Some sharks lose more than 50,000 teeth over their lifetime.

  4. Sharks blush when they're happy.

ANSWERS
1. fact 2. fiction 3. fact 4. fiction

Most sharks are solitary creatures. Some sharks 7
swim in small groups. 11

Reefs are like densely populated undersea cities. 18
This makes them great places for sharks to find meals. 28

Sharks eat fish, shellfish, squid, turtles, plankton, 35
and marine mammals. 38

Unlike most animals, sharks can move both their 46
upper and lower jaws. 50

Some shark's teeth are replaced about every eight 58
days. Certain species lose more than 50,000 teeth 66
during their lifetime. 69

Sharks are often accompanied by suckerfish, called 76
remoras, that latch onto the shark's body. 83

The whale shark is the largest fish. Although it has 93
about 300 rows of tiny teeth, it is harmless to humans. 104

Remoras attach themselves to sharks for transport, 111
protection, and an occasional free meal. They often eat 120
parasites that harm sharks. 124

Clark is a small, young shark in a very big
ocean. Everywhere he looks, he sees other fish
frolicking and playing games together. But Clark
doesn't have any friends. He feels awfully lonely.

As Clark passes a coral reef, he sees a lone
clown fish nervously poking its head out of a
crevice. Clark gathers his courage and swims
over to introduce himself. "Hello, my name is
Clark. Will you be my friend?" Clark asks
cheerfully.

"Most certainly not! I would never befriend a
shark. One minute we'd be playfully romping
about the reef, the next minute I'd wind up in
your belly! No, that just wouldn't do," the clown
fish declares as he ducks back inside his home.

Clark feels dejected, but he's still determined
to find a friend. "Maybe I should smile more," he
thinks. Clark shyly makes his way over to a
school of tuna and gives them his biggest smile.

10
18
25
33
43
52
59
67
75
76
84
91
101
110
119
126
136
145
154

22

But at the sight of Clark's wide-open mouth filled 164
with rows of terribly sharp teeth, the horrified tuna 173
dart off without even a simple good-bye! 181

"Hmm," Clark thinks, "maybe I'm just not meant 189
to have friends." But just then, a small, perky fish 199
swims right up to Clark and blurts out, "Hi, my 209
name's Laura Remora. Do you want to be my 218
friend?" 219

Clark blushes with delight. "Really? I'd love to be 228
your friend, Laura. My name's Clark." This time he 237
tries to smile without showing his teeth so he won't 247
frighten his new friend. 251

"Don't worry," Laura says. "You don't seem so 259
scary to me. I bet you're the most delightful shark 269
in the whole ocean!" 273

"Thanks," Clark responds. "It's so nice to finally 281
have a good friend. If you hop on my back, I'll take 293
you on a fantastic ride around the reef!" 301

GLOSSARY

caribou. a large, North American reindeer

clown fish. a brightly colored tropical fish that lives near sea anemones

dejected. being depressed or sad

parasite. an organism that lives and feeds on or in a different organism without contributing to the host's survival

perky. self-confident and cheerful

plankton. microscopic organisms, such as algae, that drift in water and are eaten by fish

shellfish. an aquatic animal that has a hard shell, such as a clam or lobster

species. a group of related living beings

To see a complete list of SandCastle™ books and other nonfiction titles from ABDO Publishing Company, visit www.abdopub.com or contact us at: 4940 Viking Drive, Edina, Minnesota 55435 • 1-800-800-1312 • fax: 1-952-831-1632